What Makes You Giggle?

By P.J. Shaw
Illustrated by Tom Brannon

Dalmatian Press, LLC, 2007. All rights reserved. 1-866-418-2572
Published by Dalmatian Press, LLC, 2007. The DALMATIAN PRESS name and logo are trademarks of Dalmatian Press, LLC, Franklin, Tennessee 37067. No part of this book may be reproduced or copied in any form without written permission from the copyright owner.

Printed in the U.S.A.
ISBN: 1-40373-232-9 (X)

09 10 11 12 B&M 34955 13 12 11 10
15755 Sesame Street 8x8 Storybook: What Makes You Giggle?

What makes you giggle,
What gives you a grin?
Big Bird in a tutu doing a spin!

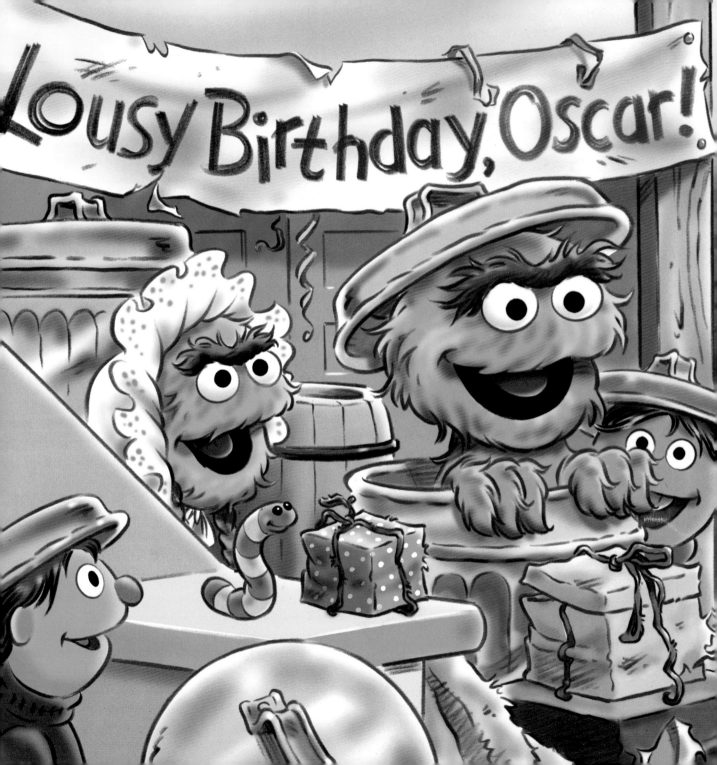

What makes you chuckle,
Or tickles your tummy?
A grouch birthday party—
Where presents are crummy!

Do giraffes give you laughs
On a trip to the zoo?
Or how about chimps?
Monkey-see, monkey-do!

A Snuffleupagus race
Might just give you a smile.
They *galumph* to the finish.
Alice wins by a mile!

What makes you laugh,
What makes you giggle?
A monstrous contest
For noses that wiggle!

Halloween's fun…
And so spooky, you shriek!

Hide-and-seek, trick-or-treat,
Oscar's can—EEK!

What makes you whoop,
Makes you squeal with delight?
A day at the pool,
When the water's just right.

Dive rings and water wings,
Snorkels and masks.
Flippers and floaties,
And fountains that splash!

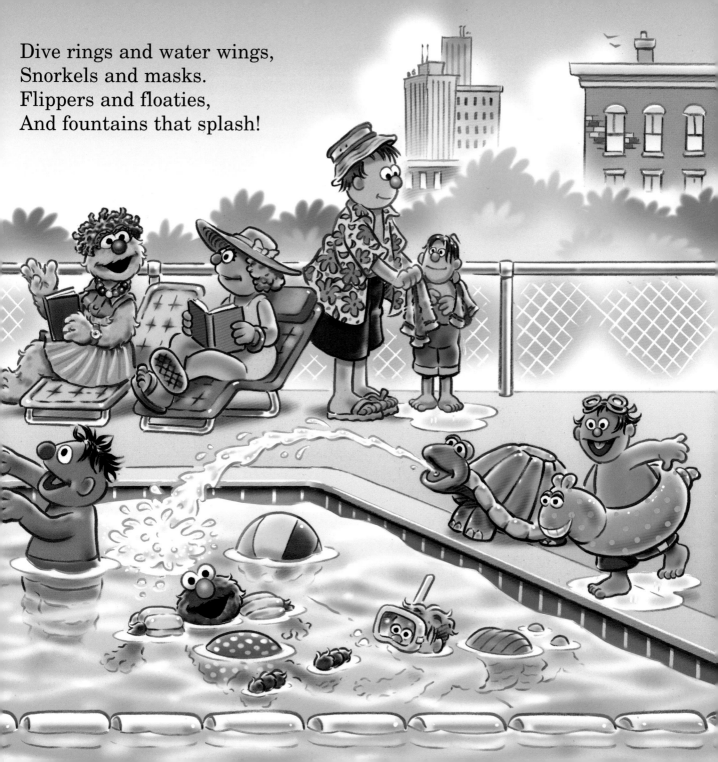

What makes you snicker,
Guffaw or tee-hee?
A neighborhood cookout
At Nani Bird's tree?

Make-your-own cupcakes
With milk-chocolate chips?
Maybe strawberries, raisins,
Or cinnamon bits....

Coconut, sprinkles,
Or butterscotch drops,
And pink-and-white frosting
To plop right on top.

What makes you goofy?
What makes you titter?
To trade silly faces
With Curly Bear's sitter!

A Twiddlebugs' picnic
With muffins and honey?

Or...an all-Grover rodeo—
Now, *that* would be funny!

What makes you giggle—
Makes you feel really good?
Just a regular day,
In your own neighborhood!